# CLIFFORD'S HICCUPS

**Adapted by Suzanne Weyn**

**Illustrated by Carolyn Bracken
and Sandrina Kurtz**

Based on the Scholastic book series
"Clifford The Big Red Dog"
by Norman Bridwell

From the television script
"Clifford's Hiccups"
by Baz Hawkins

**Cartwheel**
·B·O·O·K·S·®

## SCHOLASTIC INC.

New York  Toronto  London  Auckland  Sydney  Mexico City
New Delhi  Hong Kong

ISBN 0-439-28337-X

Library of Congress Cataloging-in-Publication Data available

10 9 8 7 6                    01 02 03 04 05

Printed in the U.S.A.
First printing, September 2001

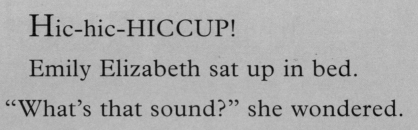

Hic-hic-HICCUP!

Emily Elizabeth sat up in bed.

"What's that sound?" she wondered.

Hic-hic-HICCUP!

Up popped the teddy bear. Up popped the doll. And up popped Emily Elizabeth. Clifford had the hiccups!

Emily Elizabeth went down to breakfast.
Hic-hic-HICCUP!

Up popped the plates and cups. Up
popped the orange juice—right onto
Mr. Howard's head!

"Maybe the vet can help Clifford," said Mrs. Howard.

Dr. Dihn checked Clifford's breathing.

"Clifford just has a case of the hiccups,"
Dr. Dihn said. "Sooner or later, they will go
away."

Outside the doctor's office, Clifford
saw his friends T-Bone and Mac.
Hic-hic-HICCUP!

"I know how to make Clifford's hiccups go away," T-Bone said to Mac. "I'll give him a little scare."

"Boo!" T-Bone shouted.

But Clifford's hiccups did not go away.

"I know how to make your hiccups
go away," Mac said to Clifford.
"Follow me!"

Mac led Clifford to a kiddie pool.
"Shut your eyes, hold your ears, then
turn upside down, and DRINK!" said Mac.

So Clifford shut his eyes, held his ears,
turned upside down, and DRANK when...

"Boo!"

T-Bone jumped out of the pool!

And Clifford's hiccups stopped!

"I did it!" said T-Bone.

"I did it!" said Mac.

Hic-hic-HICCUP!

T-Bone and Mac were very disappointed.

"We really wanted to help," said T-Bone.

"You *did* help," said Clifford. "You didn't make my hiccups go away, but I feel good because you tried so hard."

Just then, Emily Elizabeth came by.
"How are your hiccups?" she asked.

Everyone listened. Then they listened
some more.

Clifford's hiccups were finally gone!